Let brotherly love continue.
Be not forgetful to entertain strangers:
For thereby some have entertained
angels unawares.

HEBREWS 13:1,2

for Madeline

WALKER BOOKS
AND SUBSIDIARIES
LONDON · BOSTON · SYDNEY · AUCKLAND

First published 2002 by Walker Books Ltd
87 Vauxhall Walk, London SE11 5HJ

This edition published 2004

10 9 8 7 6 5 4

© 2002 Bob Graham

The right of Bob Graham to be identified
as author/illustrator of this work has been
asserted by him in accordance with the
Copyright, Designs and Patents Act 1988

This book has been typeset in
Stempel Schneidler medium

Printed in China

British Library Cataloguing in Publication Data:
a catalogue record for this book is available
from the British Library

ISBN 978-1-84428-482-5

www.walkerbooks.co.uk

DISCO

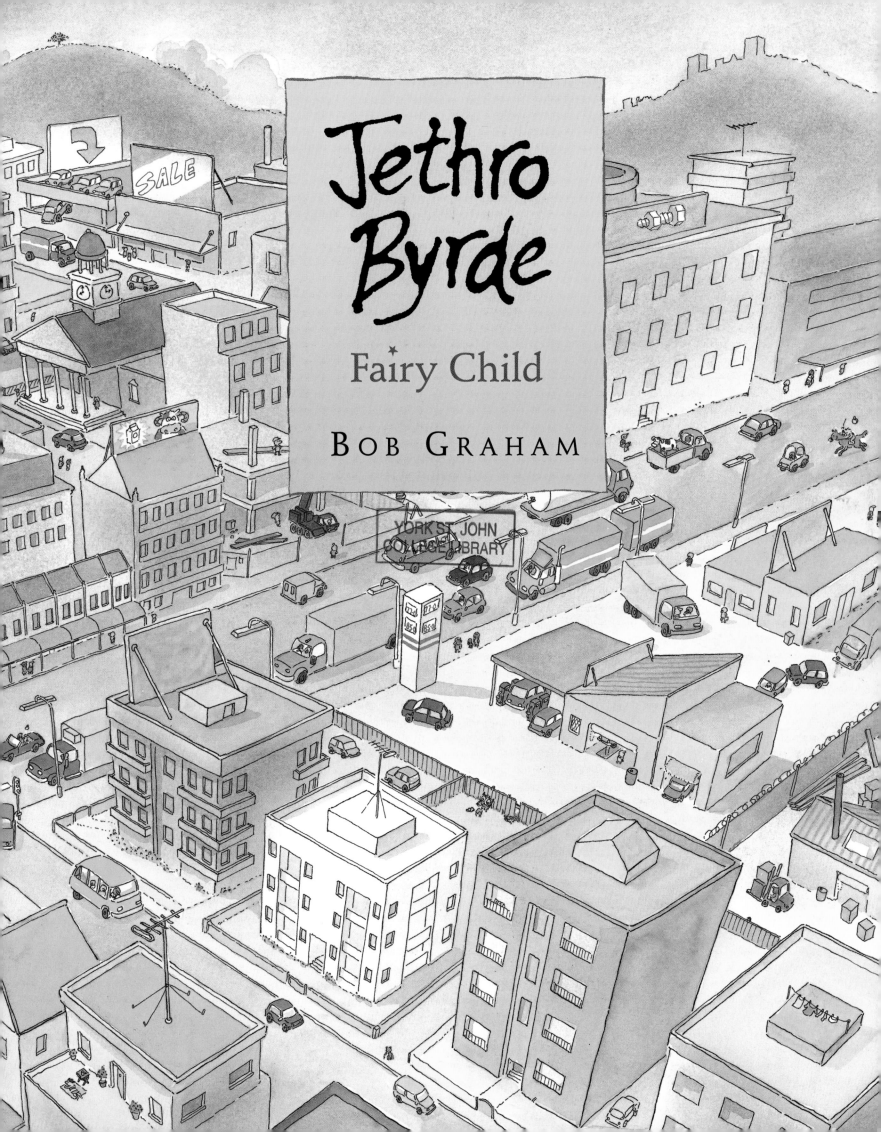

Jethro Byrde

★ Fairy Child

BOB GRAHAM

Annabelle's dad had little time for fairies.
"Sadly, Annie," he said, "you won't
find fairies in cement and weeds –
so far as I know."

Annabelle had lots of time, and
every day she looked.

Even under her brother, Sam.

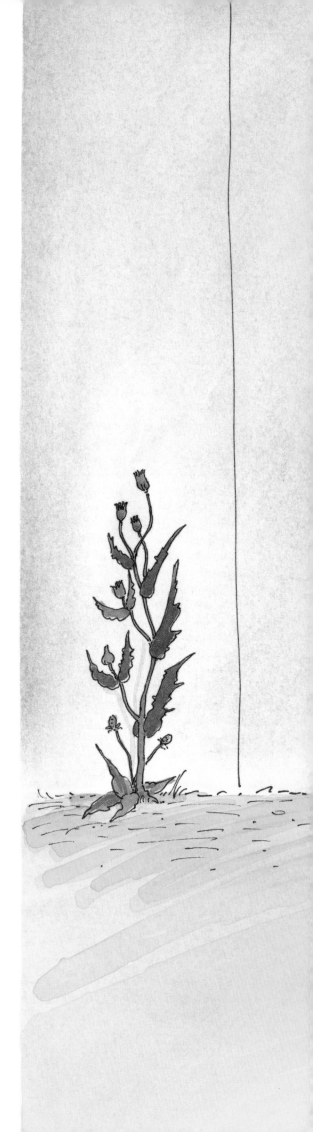

On Saturday,
    something bounced off the
service station driveway and hit the fence,
    just where the weeds poked through. Annabelle parked her taxi.
And, with the fares uncollected, she went through to see.

There she met a boy –

as big as her finger.

His wings shivered in the breeze.

"Who are *you*?" she said.

He hitched up his jeans,

flew onto a leaf and wiped his nose

on the back of his sleeve.

"Jethro," he said. "Jethro Byrde ... I'm a *Fairy Child.*"

What Annabelle saw next made her hold her breath.
A roadside hot dog van had dropped from the
sky and lay among the bottles and cans.
A family of fairies heaved
and pushed.

"Help us here will you please?"
came a voice from the weeds.
Annabelle gently put out
her hand to set the van
back on its wheels.

"Thanks," said the voice.
"And to whom do we owe
      this pleasure?"
Jethro's dad, Offin Byrde,
bowed deeply from the waist.
"He means, what's your name?"
      said Jethro.
"Annabelle," Annabelle said.

She let out her breath,
making Jethro's mum's hair
ripple like grass in a windy field.
"What a lovely name,"
said Lily Byrde. She kissed
Annabelle on the cheek.

"That was one of Offin's
not-so-good landings,"
said Grandma Byrde.
"Nearly hit the top of the
service station," added Lily.

Offin looked cross.
"Well we all agreed to come
down for tea," said Offin.

"And to feed baby Cecily,"
said Lily. Cecily was as
big as a fingernail.

"My mum will make you tea," Annabelle said.

Lily's bells and bangles tinkled round her ankles.

"We would *love* to come to tea," she said.

"Let's go," said Jethro.

He did a Backward Air Skid over the fence.

"Mummy and Daddy, this is Jethro Byrde. He's a Fairy Child, and his family have come to tea," said Annabelle.
"We must make them welcome, *and* make them tea," said Mum.

But she was looking the wrong way.

"Can you see Jethro, Daddy?"
Annabelle asked.
"I ... I think I can, Annie.
I think he's ...
ON THE FENCE?"

"Why doesn't my dad see you?"
Annabelle asked Lily.
"He's too grown up,
   Annabelle,"
      she replied.
"He doesn't have time for fairies."

"Do *you* have time for fairies, Mummy?"
         Annabelle asked.

            "I've got time to make your friends
               tea," replied Mum. "Or maybe
                  they have a magic wand?"

            "Can you make magic?"
            Annabelle asked.
            The Byrdes shook their heads.
            "We just make hamburgers,"
               said Offin Byrde.

Annabelle's mum
brought fairy cakes
and camomile tea
in fairy cups.

Annabelle gave cake to
all her guests.
"Your mum's cakes are
charming," said Lily.
"Enchanting," said Grandma.
"Magic," said Offin.

They had second helpings and
refilled their cups with tea.

Only Annabelle's dad left his tea
untouched. His fingers moved
over his keyboard.

Clickety click,
clickety click,
clickety click.

Offin Byrde's foot began to tap.
He wiped his fingers and
reached for his bag.

Inside was a tiny fiddle,
dark red-brown like a chestnut.
As his bow hit the strings,
his fingers started flying.

That afternoon, for Annabelle,
time stood still.

Offin played reels and he played jigs.
Lily danced with her charms and bracelets
tinkling like windchimes.

Jethro played a silver whistle,
his sneakers sliding
in cake crumbs.

Baby Cecily slept soundly,
while Grandma sang a
slow, sad song,
clear as a church bell.

"No one sings sweeter
than a fairy," said Offin.
"Unless it's the lark
in the morning,"
Grandma replied.

"Maybe Jethro could stay with *me*?" Annabelle said.

"We need you, Jethro," said Lily, "to help make the ice creams."

"And his aunts. They'll want to see Jethro again. It's been a whole year," said Grandma.

"Last year you won a beautiful plastic cup," said Offin.

Jethro sulked a bit. Then he said,

"Maybe Annabelle could come with *us*?"

"I would love to come," said Annabelle.

"*Pleeease* take me with you."

Annabelle waited. The Byrde family whispered together.

Finally, Jethro took something off his wrist.

It sparkled silver in the late sun.

"It's for you, Annabelle," Offin said. "A fairy watch telling fairy time."

"And time goes slowly by for fairies," said Grandma.

"We thank you, Annabelle," said Lily, "for being kind and caring…"

"To strangers like us," added Grandma.

"And for the fairy cakes," said Jethro.

"We're sorry we can't take you with us," Lily went on.

"But fairies are this size, and humans are …
well, you're just too big."

"Will you come again?" Annabelle asked.
The fairy watch fitted exactly round her finger.
"I'm sure we will," Jethro replied,
"just don't forget to wind the watch."
"And keep looking," said Lily.
Annabelle carefully put the
van on the driveway.

The engine coughed
and spluttered.
Wild flowers burst from the tailpipe.
And for those who had time to look,
the small van gathered speed.
It bumped over the cracks in the concrete
and slowly left the ground like
a swan in flight.
The van cleared the service station roof and
headed out west into the gathering dusk.

"Look at my ring, Daddy.
It's a fairy watch telling fairy time,"
said Annabelle.
"That's lovely, Annie," replied her dad.
He saw nothing, but Baby Sam did.
His fingers left cake and icing
on the glass.

"The Byrdes said they were the nicest
fairy cakes they have ever eaten, Mummy," said Annabelle.
"Oh, *thank you*, Annabelle," replied her mum.

"I did find fairies in our cement and weeds, Mummy,"
said Annabelle.

And that night, the watch strapped tightly round her finger,
Annabelle saw more fairies.

From rich houses, poor houses,
caravans and car parks, from under wood heaps
and high up in blackbirds' nests, from churches and
shop windows and department stores after dark,
from mountains and valleys, back streets
and motorways, from under hedges and bridges,
they rode in the moonlight to
the Fairy Travellers' Picnic.

And long after she fell asleep, their busy chattering
and the buzzing of their wings and their
faraway music filled her dreams.